Special Thanks

To my family: *Shaun, Katie, Erin, and Lauren for your wonderful ideas; to Ruthann Hendrickson and Don Greene for your puckish sense of fun and great joy in life; to my nephews, Benjamin and Jordan Bendiburg, for making your tia laugh; and to Mami and Papi, of course.*

To media specialists: *Lorry de la Croix, Jane Sullivan, Sherry des Enfants, Harriet Brown, Martha Hooper, Rita Linker, Julie Strickland, Betty Beasley, Karen Haglund, Carol Harless, Betty Brown, Ellen Limbrick, and the Miss Lottys of the Norcross Public Library.*

— C.D.

Thanks to my wife, Traci, to my mother,
and to all my family and friends for your belief in my work.

— M.W.

Published by

PEACHTREE PUBLISHERS, LTD.
1700 Chattahoochee Avenue
Atlanta, Georgia 30318-2112

Text © 1994 by Carmen Agra Deedy
Illustrations © 1994 by Michael P. White

Book design and composition by Nicola Simmonds Carter
Production Supervision by Loraine M. Balcsik

10 9
Manufactured in Singapore

Library of Congress Cataloging-in-Publication Data

Deedy, Carmen Agra.
The library dragon / Carmen Agra Deedy: illustrated by Michael P. White.
p. cm.
Summary: Miss Lotta Scales is a dragon who believes her job is to protect the school's library books from the children, but when she finally realizes that books are meant to be read, the dragon turns into Miss Lotty, librarian and storyteller.

ISBN 1-56145-091-X : $16.95

[1. Librarians—Fiction. 2. Dragons—Fiction. 3. Libraries —Fiction. 4. Books and reading—Fiction. 5. Schools—Fiction.]
I. White, Michael P., ill. II. Title.
PZ7.D3587Li 1994
[E]—dc20
94-14754
CIP
AC

The Library Dragon

CARMEN AGRA DEEDY

ILLUSTRATED BY
MICHAEL
P. WHITE

PEACHTREE
ATLANTA

This book is dedicated to Cherrie Smith, who has known all along that in the library beats the heart of the school.

And to Robin DeFoe, who is like a sister.

— C.D.

To my father, who taught me that the true meaning of a man is not power or strength, but how he treats all people. I miss you.

— M.W.

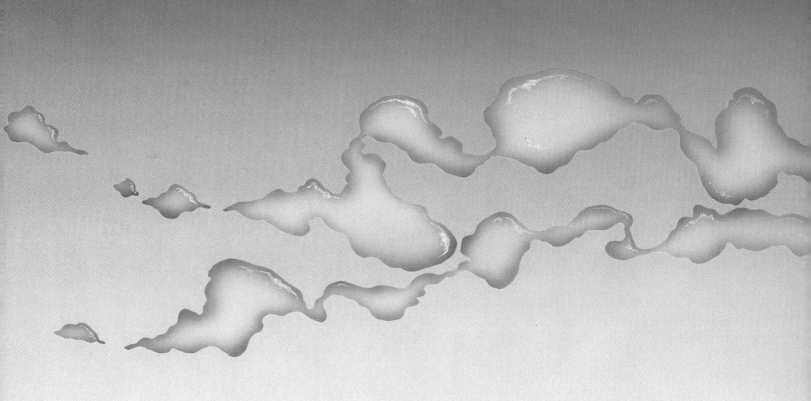

Sunrise Elementary School had a BIG problem.
The new librarian, Miss Lotta Scales, was a *real dragon*.

Miss Lotta Scales was hired to guard the Library.
And she took her job seriously: hundreds of new, clean
books replaced the old, smudged ones. These shining
gems neatly lined the shelves of her library lair in perfect
order — no 398.2s in the 500s, and absolutely no fiction
among the biographies.

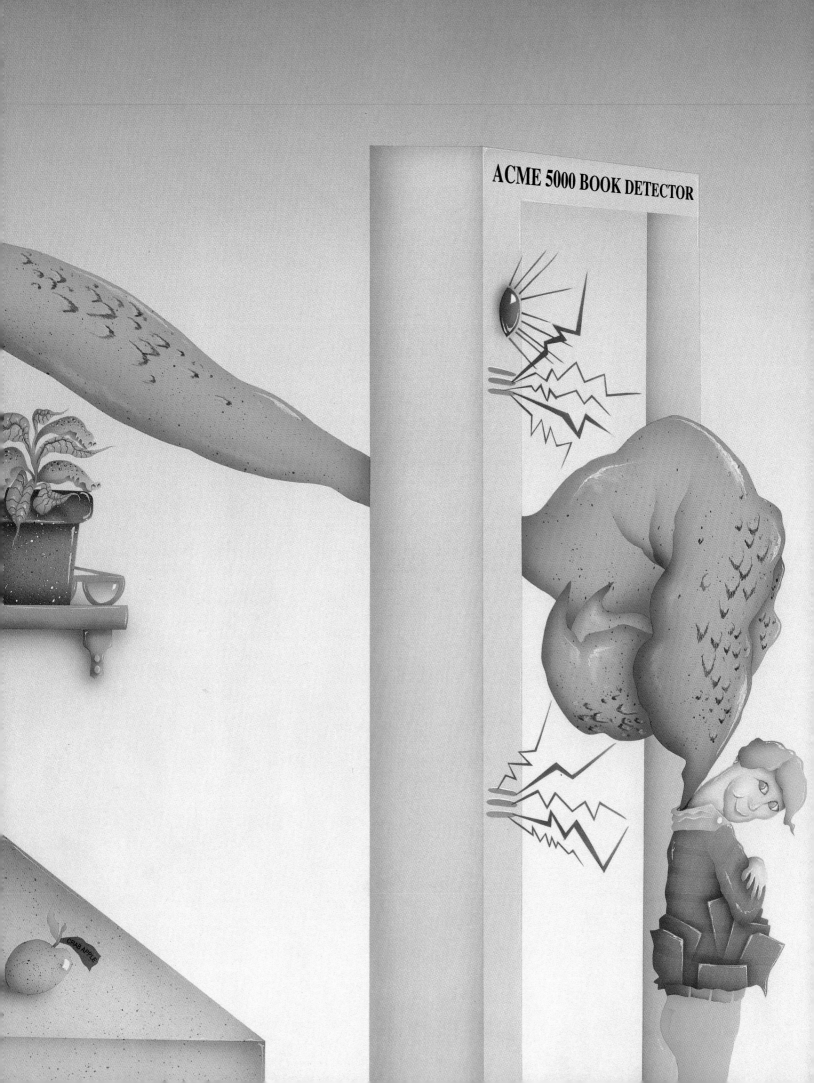

She kept a fiery eye out to make sure no one removed
any books from the shelves. Her motto was,
    "A place for everything, and that's where it *stays.*"
The very thought of sticky little fingers

touching
and
clutching,

pawing
and
clawing,

smearing
and
tearing

her precious books just made her hot under the collar.

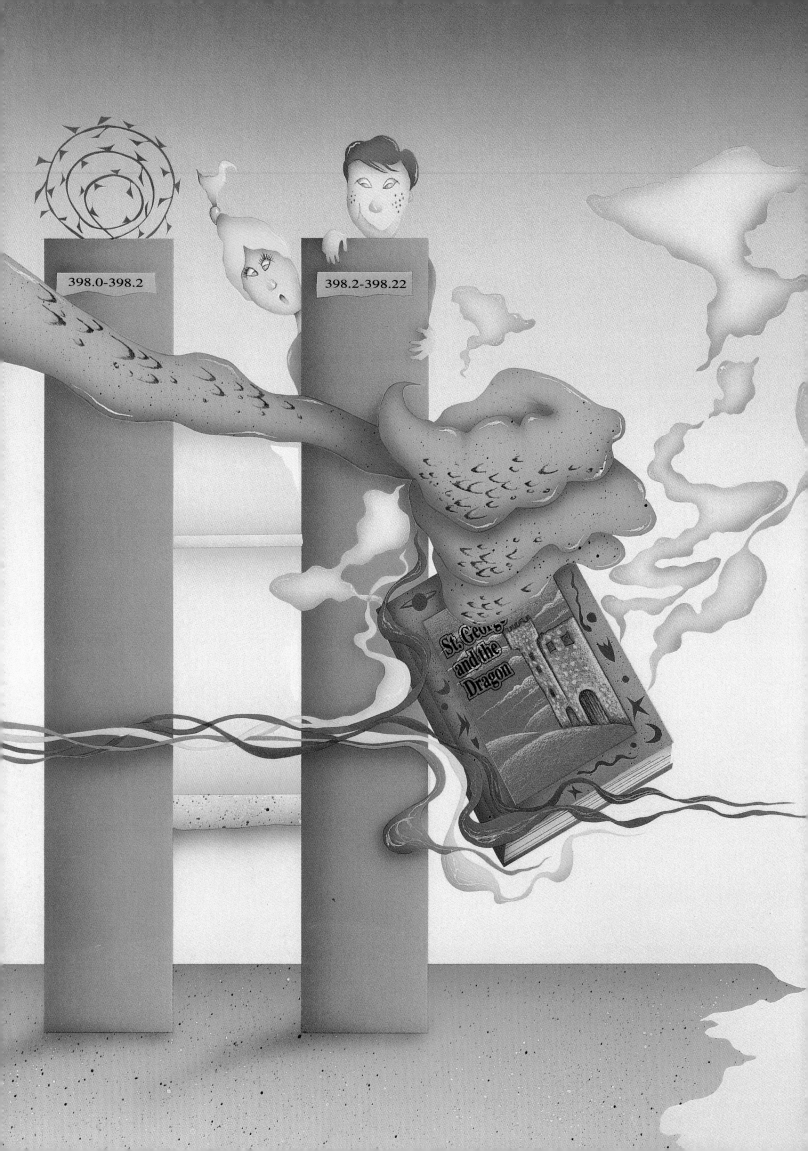

Miss Scales thought that the way some books spread an unfounded fear of dragons was positively inflammatory.

"Books that depict cruelty to dragons should never have been published in the first place."

She got so fired up about this, she didn't just discard the books she didn't like, she *incinerated* them.

The kids watched in awe.

"Well, that settles it," whispered Albert Hoops. "Where there's smoke, there's fire, and that Miss Scales is a *real dragon*, all right."

DRAGON LINE · DO NOT CROSS · DRAGON LINE · DO

 **IF ALARMED,
PULL TAIL**

Not surprisingly, the kids at Sunrise Elementary
School began to dread Library Day.

It wasn't long before the teachers stopped sending
the children to the Library: they kept coming back singed.

LINE - DO NOT CROSS -

ATTENTION NON-DRAGONS
NO SMOKING
IN THE LIBRARY

PRINCIPAL
LANCE SHIELDS

First, the principal tried
to reason with Miss Scales,
but his plan backfired.
Instead of cooling her down,
he just fanned the flames.

"And finally, don't forget who does the hiring, Miss
Scales," sputtered the principal.

"Oh really? And who does the *firing*?" asked Miss Scales
with a glare and a flare that caught his tie on fire.

"Now cut that out," said the principal as he waved the
smoke out of his face.

"No smoking in the Library," Miss Lotta Scales said drily.

The principal fumed. The teachers were incensed. Worst of all,
the children had missed reading and storytime for weeks and their
grades were going up in smoke.

So, the teachers formed a delegation. And after a trip to the
cafeteria kitchen to fortify themselves, they paid a visit to Miss Scales.

ACME WELDING CO

Jalapeño Kabob

ACME FIREPROOF LUNCHBOX

ACME SUPPLY CATALOG · DRAGON EDITION

POMPEII HOT SAUCE Lava Strength

Miss Lotta Scales smouldered as she listened to sweet Miss Lemon the kindergarten teacher.

"…and most importantly, Miss Scales, dear, the children miss storytime."

"Storytime, shmorie-time," blew Miss Lotta Scales, "why, if I let the children touch these books with their gooey fingers and snotty noses, this Library wouldn't last a week."

And she stared so furiously at the teachers that they threw down their weapons and clanged out. All except sweet Miss Lemon.

"You know, Miss Scales, we all love the books as much as you do…, but *the Library belongs to the children.*"

"Good Knight, Miss Lemon, you slay me," cracked Miss Scales. "Why the idea of storytime is simply *medieval.*"

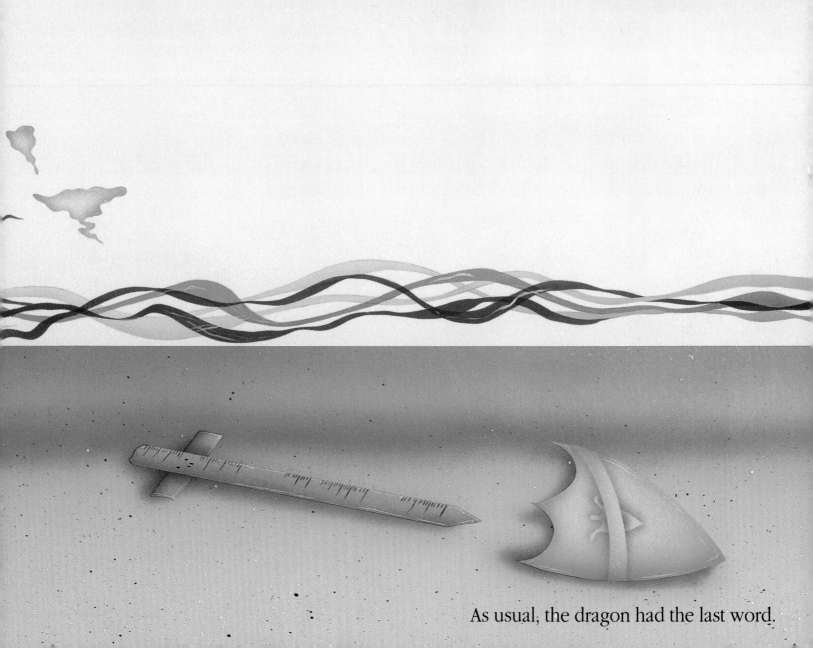

As usual, the dragon had the last word.

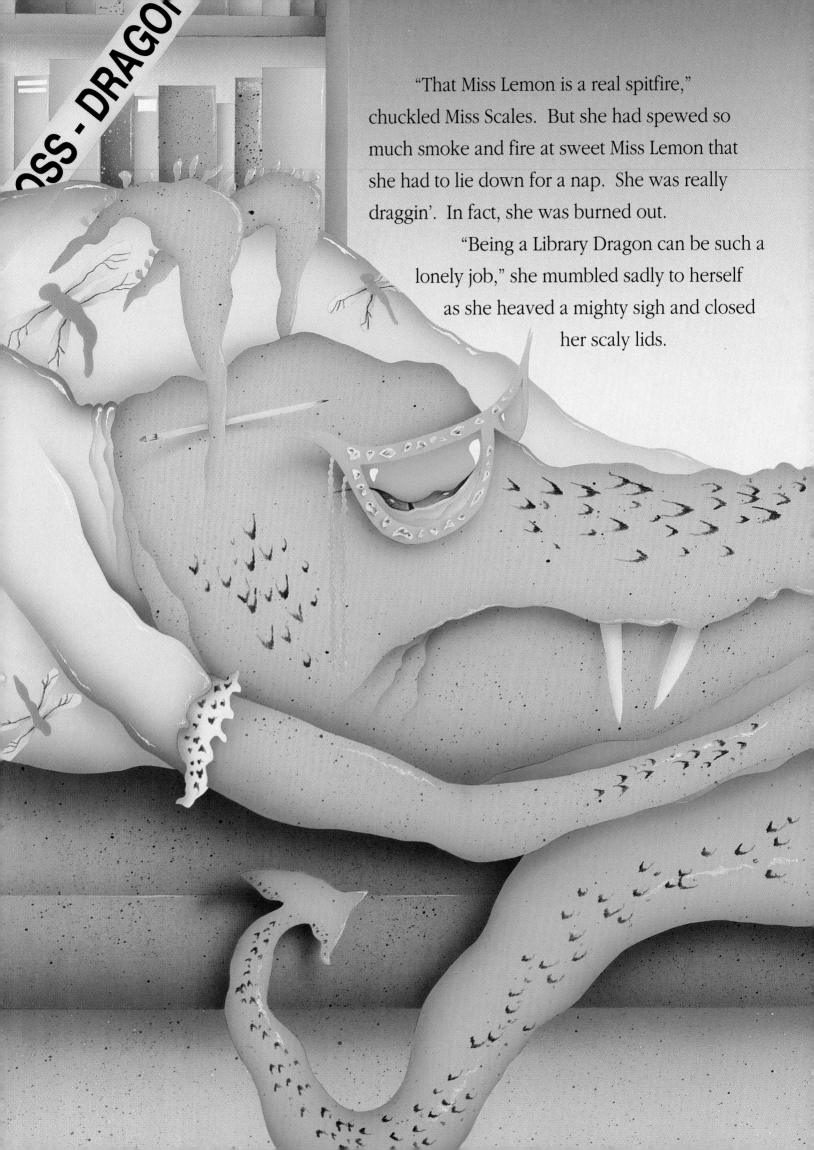

"That Miss Lemon is a real spitfire," chuckled Miss Scales. But she had spewed so much smoke and fire at sweet Miss Lemon that she had to lie down for a nap. She was really draggin'. In fact, she was burned out.

"Being a Library Dragon can be such a lonely job," she mumbled sadly to herself as she heaved a mighty sigh and closed her scaly lids.

It was at that very moment that Molly Brickmeyer
accidentally wandered into the Library.

CRAB APPLE

Snuff The Magic Dragon

Molly was on a quest: she had lost her glasses and couldn't see a thing without them unless it was right under her nose. She stumbled into a bookshelf and a book fell onto her lap. She never saw the sign that read,

**Do Not Touch The Books
For Display Only**

It was over her head.
So she held this one right under her nose
and began to read out loud.

First a class of second graders, in line for the water fountain, heard her and tiptoed in to listen.
Then, the fourth graders, outside playing kickball, heard a story being read and crowded around the windows.

"Speak up," someone said.
Molly Brickmeyer spoke up.
Word of storytime in the Library spread like wildfire at Sunrise Elementary School.

Everyone
was listening.
Even the
Library Dragon.

And her ears
were burning.

Slowly Miss Lotta Scales rose up from behind a
bookshelf and looked at the boys and girls huddled around
Molly. She'd never seen anything quite like it: *the children
looked like they belonged here.*

"'…I love you, Snuff,'" Molly read on as all the
children listened.

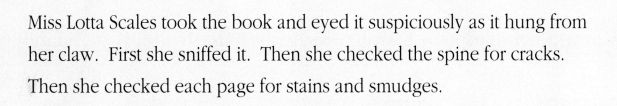

"Give me that book, Molly Brickmeyer," roared Miss Scales.

Molly held the book cheerfully toward the scaly blur.

Miss Lotta Scales took the book and eyed it suspiciously as it hung from her claw. First she sniffed it. Then she checked the spine for cracks. Then she checked each page for stains and smudges.

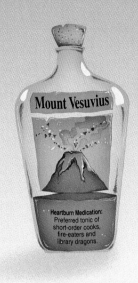

Mount Vesuvius

Heartburn Medication:
Preferred tonic of
short-order cooks,
fire-eaters and
library dragons.

Finally Miss Scales looked around at the children and cleared the smoke from her throat.

"Now, where were we? Why, yes, … 'I love you, Snuff…'"

At first the children were too nervous to listen. But when Molly Brickmeyer climbed up onto Miss Lotta Scales's lap—and didn't get scorched—they relaxed.

"You're warm," whispered Molly.
"Don't interrupt," Miss Scales crackled.

Everyone was listening so intently that they almost missed it: as she read, Miss Lotta Scales's scales began to fall on the linoleum floor with a clickety-clack, clickety-clack, . . .

…clickety-clack—until all that was left was Miss Lotty, librarian and storyteller, sitting on a mountain of yellow, green, and purple scales with Molly Brickmeyer, Dragon Slayer Extraordinaire, on her lap.

The rest of the children warmed up to Miss Lotty right away.

The changes in Miss Lotty's new kid-friendly library
were hard to miss. Not surprisingly, the kids at Sunrise
Elementary School began to *love* Library Day.

Miss Lotty's transformation, however,
was not complete . . .

But then, every librarian needs to be a little bit of a dragon —
or else,
WHO WOULD GUARD THE BOOKS?

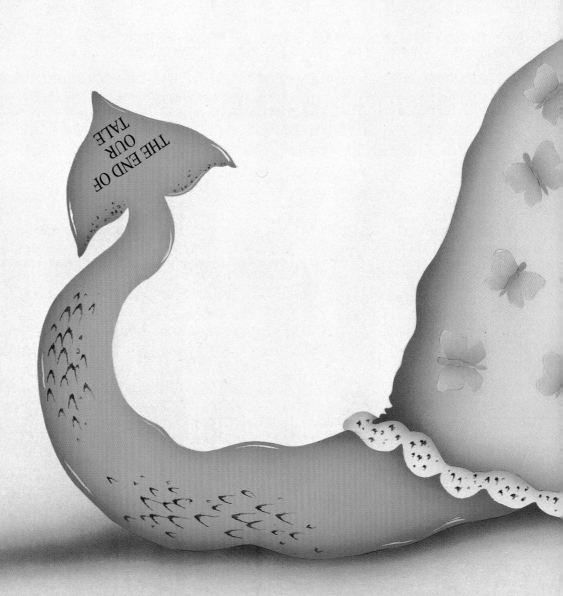

THE END OF
OUR
TALE